Thesaurus Rex

Written by Laya Steinberg
Illustrated by Debbie Harter

Barefoot Books
Celebrating Art and Story

Thesaurus Rex drinks his milk:
sip, sup, swallow, swill.

whoops!
He's had a
messy spill.

Thesaurus Rex goes exploring:

hunting,

searching,

and romp.

wow! He's found a muddy swamp.

Thesaurus Rex lands in mud:
slime, slush, mire and muck.

Oh no! Now he's stuck.

Thesaurus Rex must get clean:

wash,

bathe,

scour

and scrub.

He's left footprints
in the tub.

Thesaurus Rex is ready to eat:
  munch, crunch, nibble, gnaw.

Chomp!
He likes his
dinner raw.

Thesaurus Rex is all wrapped up:
bundled,
covered,
tucked in tight.

He'll have happy
dreams tonight.
Goodnight!

Barefoot Books
2067 Massachusetts Ave
Cambridge, MA 02140

First hardcover edition published in the United States of America in 2003 by Barefoot Books, Inc.
This paperback edition published 2005. All rights reserved. No part of this book may be reproduced in any
form or by any means, electronic or mechanical, including photocopying, recording or by any information
storage and retrieval system, without permission in writing from the publisher

This book was typeset in Bokka
The illustrations were prepared in watercolor, pen and ink and crayon on thick watercolor paper

Graphic design by Big Blu Ltd.
Color separation by Grafiscan, Italy
Printed and bound in China by Printplus Ltd.
This book has been printed on 100% acid-free paper

13 15 17 19 20 18 16 14 12

Library of Congress Cataloging-in-Publication Data

Steinberg, Laya.
    Thesaurus Rex / written by Laya Steinberg ; illustrated by Debbie Harter.
        p. cm.
    Summary: Thesaurus Rex's misadventurous day is described
    in a variety of synonyms.
    ISBN 1-84148-180-7 (pbk. : alk. paper) [1. Dinosaurs--Fiction.
    2. English language--Synonyms and antonyms--Fiction. 3.
    Humorous stories. 4. Stories in rhyme.] I. Harter, Debbie, ill.
        II. Title.
                    PZ8.3.S8195Th 2005
                    [E]--dc22
                                    2004017898